Within the fairy-tale treasure which has come into the world's possession, there is no doubt Hans Christian Andersen's stories are of outstanding character. Their symbolism is rich with Christian values, and some of them are clear illustrations of the Gospel. From his early childhood in the town of Odense, Denmark, until his death in Copenhagen, Hans Christian Andersen (1805-1875) had a valid Christian faith that manifested itself in many of the approximately 150 stories and tales he wrote. In one of them, he said: "In every human life, whether poor or great, there is an invisible thread that shows we belong to God." The thread in Andersen's stories is one of optimism which has given hope and inspiration to people all over the world.

It is in this spirit that the Tales of Hans Christian Andersen are published. We are convinced of the validity of teaching spiritual principles and building character values through imaginative stories, just as Jesus used parables to teach the people of His time.

THE PIGKEEPER
by Hans Christian Andersen
Translated from the original Danish text by
Terence Andrew Day BA
Illustrated by Francois Crozat
U.S. Edition 1988 by WORD Inc. Waco.TX 76702
Text: © Copyright 1987 Scandinavia Publishing House,
Nørregade 32, DK-1165, Copenhagen K. Denmark
Artwork: © Copyright 1987 Francois Crozat and
Scandinavia Publishing House
Printed in Hong Kong
ISBN 0-8499-8543-9

Hans Christian Andersen

The Pigkeeper

Illustrated by Francois Crozat
Translated for children from the original Danish text
by Terence Andrew Day BA

WORD INC.

Once upon a time there lived a poor prince. He had a kingdom that was rather small, but still it was large enough for him to afford to marry, and he wanted to get married.

Now it was really rather brave of him, daring to go up to the Emperor's daughter and ask, "Do you want me or not?" But he dared because his name was famous far and wide. There were hundreds of princesses who would have said, "yes please." But let's see whether or not this one did.

On the gravestone of the prince's father there grew a rosebush, and what a beautiful rosebush it was! It only blossomed every five years and even then bore just one flower. But that one rose had a perfume so sweet, anyone smelling it immediately forgot all their worries and cares.

The prince also had a nightingale which could sing as if every lovely tune in the world lived inside its little throat.

CI-GIT
ONESIME-FÉLICIEN DÉSIRÉ
DE LA TOUR-DIT JOJO XXVII

The princess was to have the rose and the nightingale, and so they were put into two large silver cases and sent to her.

The Emperor had the gifts brought in before him in the great hall where the princess was playing cards with her ladies-in-waiting. That was all they ever did, so when she caught sight of the large cases with the gifts inside, she clapped her hands for joy.

"Oh, I do hope it's a little pussycat!" she said. And then the beautiful rose was taken out.

"Oooh! Look at how lovely it's made!" said all the ladies-in-waiting.

"It's more than lovely!" said the Emperor. "It's nice!"

But then the princess touched it and burst into tears.

"Ugh! Papa!" she said. "It's not fake, it's real!"

"Ugh!" echoed all the people at the court. "It's real!"

7

"Let's first have a look what's in the other case before we get angry!" the Emperor suggested. The nightingale was taken out and it sang so beautifully that for a moment, no one could say a bad word about it.

"Superbe! Charmant!" said the ladies-in-waiting, for they all spoke French, the one more badly than the other.

"How the bird reminds me of our late lamented Empress's music box!" said an old knight. "Oh yes, definitely the same note, the same harmony!"

"Yes, you're right!" said the Emperor. And he cried like a little baby.

"Please don't tell me it's a real bird!" said the princess.

"But it is a real bird!" said the servants who had brought it in.

"Then let the thing fly away!" said the princess. Then she refused to see the prince.

11

But he was not so easily put off. He covered
his face in dirt, put on shabby clothes, pulled
a cap over his head and knocked at the gate.

"Good day, Emperor!" he said. "How about
giving me a job in your castle?"

"Well, I don't know. There are so many who
would like to work here!" said the Emperor.
"But let me see, I need someone who can look
after the pigs, we've got so many of them!"

And so the prince was made royal pigkeeper.
He was given a dark little room down by the
pigsty and there he had to stay.

But all day long he sat working and when evening
came, he had made a cute little pot with bells all
around it. Whenever the pot began to boil, the
bells tinkled so sweetly, playing the old tune:

"Oh, my darling Augustine,
All is gone, gone, gone, gone!"

But the funniest thing of all was, as soon as you held your finger above the steam coming out of the pot, you could smell all the food being cooked in all the stoves and ovens in town. That was all together something quite different than a rose.

When the princess, together with all her ladies-in-waiting, walked by the pigsty, she heard the melody.

She stood still and looked ever so delighted, for
that was the only tune she could play and that
was with just the one finger.

"Why, I know how to play that!" she said.
"He must surely be a well-educated pigkeeper!
Listen! Go in and ask him how much he wants
for the instrument."

So one of the ladies-in-waiting had to run inside, but she put on her clogs first.

"How much do you want for that pot?" asked the lady.

"I want ten kisses from the princess!" said the pigkeeper.

"Heaven preserve us!" said the lady.

"I'll not settle for less!" said the pigkeeper.

"Well, what did he say?" asked the princess.

"I really cannot tell you," replied the lady. "It was so awful!"

"Whisper it in my ear then!" And so she whispered it into the princess's ear.

"What a rude young man!" said the princess. And she walked off at once.

But no sooner had she gone a few paces, when she heard how the bells were ringing out so cheerfully:

"Oh, my darling Augustine,
All is gone, gone, gone, gone!"

"Listen," said the princess, "ask him whether he would accept ten kisses from one of my ladies-in-waiting instead!"

"No thank you!" said the pigkeeper. "Ten kisses from the princess, or I keep the pot."

"Oh, this is so embarrassing!" said the princess. "But you'll have to stand around me, so nobody can see!"

So the ladies-in-waiting lined themselves up in front of her, spreading their dresses out. Then the pigkeeper was given his ten kisses and she got her pot.

How entertaining it was! The pot was made to boil all during the evening and all through the day.

There was not a stove or oven in the whole town where they did not know exactly what was being cooked for dinner, lords and shoemakers alike. The ladies-in-waiting danced and clapped their hands for sheer delight.

"We know who's going to have pancakes and jam! We know who's having pork chops and stew! Isn't that interesting!"

"Most interesting!" said the leading lady of the court.

"Yes, but don't say a word to anyone, for I am the Emperor's daughter!"

"We promise!" they all said.

The pigkeeper, that is to say the prince, for they did not know he was not a real pigkeeper, then made a rattle. When swung, it played all the waltzes, galopps and polkas ever known since the world began.

"But that is superbe!" said the princess, as she went past, "I have never heard a finer composition! Listen! Go in and ask him what he wants for that instrument, but no kisses this time!"

"He wants a hundred kisses from the princess!" said the lady-in-waiting who had been in to ask.

"I think he must be mad!" said the princess and so she left. But she had not gone far when she stopped. "One must encourage art!" she said, "I am the Emperor's daughter, after all! Tell him he can have ten kisses like yesterday, and my ladies-in-waiting can give him the rest!"

"Yes, but we would rather not!" said all the ladies.

"Nonsense!" said the princess. "If I can kiss him, so can you. Remember, I'm the one who gives you food and wages!". And so the lady-in-waiting had to go into the pigkeeper's dingy little room again.

"A hundred kisses from the princess," he said, "or I'll keep my rattle!"

"Stand around me!!!" said the princess. So all the ladies-in-waiting placed themselves around her. Then he kissed her and kissed her and kissed her.

"What on earth is that crowd doing down there by the pigsty?" said the Emperor, who had stepped out onto his balcony. He rubbed his eyes and put on his glasses. "It's those ladies-in-waiting playing tricks again! I'd better go down and see what they are up to!" So he quickly pulled on his slippers and hurried off down to the pigsty as fast as his legs could carry him.

As soon as he reached the yard, he moved as quietly as he could. The ladies-in-waiting were so busy counting kisses and making sure all was done fair and square, he was not to have too many and not too few either, that they did not even notice the Emperor. He stood on his tiptoes to see over the ladies-in-waiting.

"What's this!" he said. When he saw that they were kissing, he threw his slipper, and hit the prince and princess on the head. This happened just as the pigkeeper was taking his eighty-sixth kiss.

"Get out!" said the Emperor, losing his temper. And so both the princess and the pigkeeper were banished from the kingdom. There she stood crying and moaning. Meanwhile the pigkeeper told her to keep quiet. And the rain came pouring down.

"Oh, what a miserable person I am!" said the princess, "If only I had taken that handsome prince! Oh, I'm so unhappy!"

Then the pigkeeper went behind a tree, washed his face clean of all the dirt, threw off his shabby clothes and appeared in his royal robes. He looked so handsome that the princess could not help bowing down before him.

The prince looked at her and shook his head. "I've learned what kind of a person you really are and I don't like you at all!" he said. "You didn't want an honest prince! You were unable to appreciate the beauty of the rose and the nightingale, but you did not mind kissing the pigkeeper for a mere toy! Now you'll just have to make the best of it!"

And so he returned to his kingdom, shut the door and shoved the bolt to lock it. And now, indeed, all the princess could do was sit outside and sing:

"Oh, my darling Augustine,
All is gone, gone, gone, gone!"

># ▄▄━● *Study Key*

The Pigkeeper

Explaining the story:

Things are not always as they seem. This story is a reminder of that which is truly important. There is a danger in choosing to make the wrong things too important. This story teaches that you should look beyond wanting to have more things, and focus instead on the true worth of people around you.

Talking about the truth of the story:

1. How did the ladies-in-waiting, emperor and princess react to the prince's gifts? What do their reactions tell us about these people?
2. Why do things seem to matter so much?
3. What did you have when you were born? What will you be able to take with you when you die?

Applying the truth of the story:

1. Is there some thing you want very, very badly? Why do you want it so much?
2. Name what you would call the really important things in your own life.